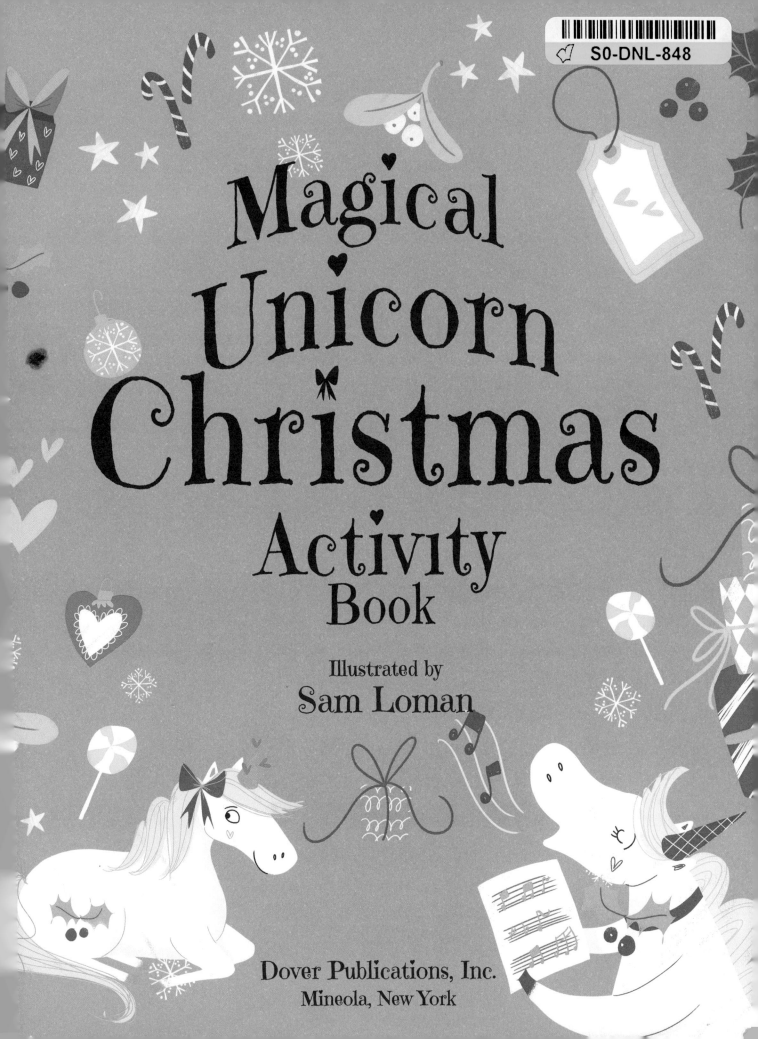

Magical
Unicorn
Christmas
Activity
Book

Illustrated by
Sam Loman

Dover Publications, Inc.
Mineola, New York

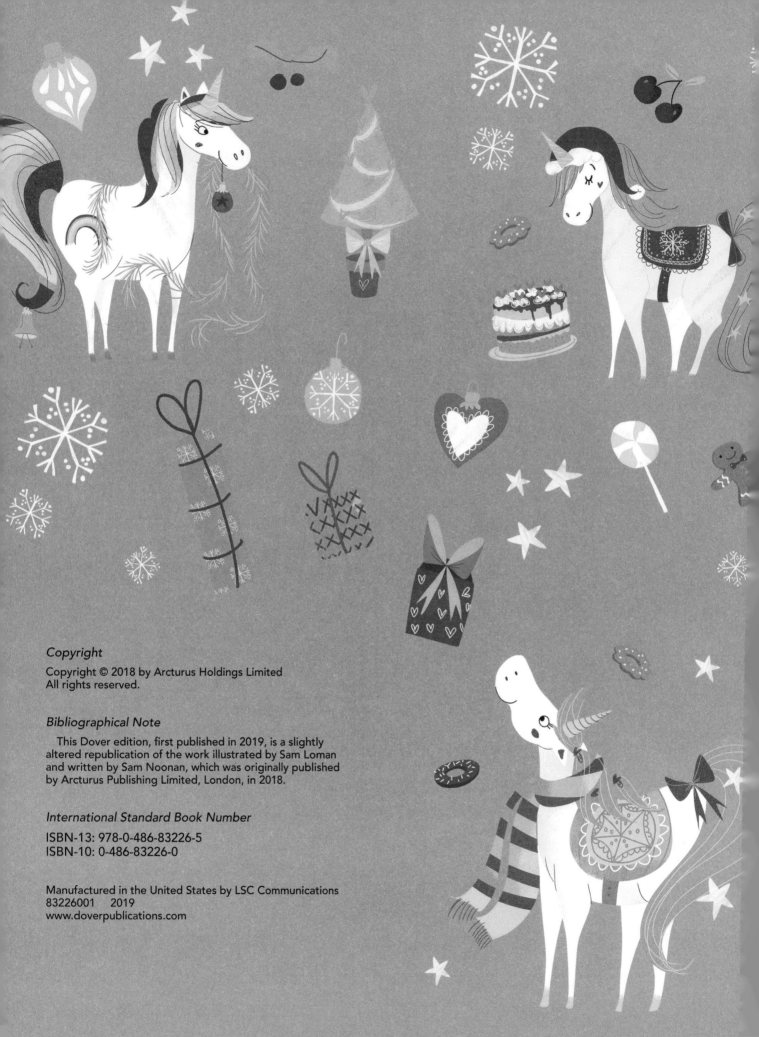

Bibliographical Note

   This Dover edition, first published in 2019, is a slightly
altered republication of the work illustrated by Sam Loman
and written by Sam Noonan, which was originally published
by Arcturus Publishing Limited, London, in 2018.

International Standard Book Number

ISBN-13: 978-0-486-83226-5
ISBN-10: 0-486-83226-0

Manufactured in the United States by LSC Communications
83226001   2019
www.doverpublications.com

Decoration Doodle

It's Christmastime in Unicorn Land and Stardust has started decorating her Christmas tree. Draw some magical decorations to help her finish it.

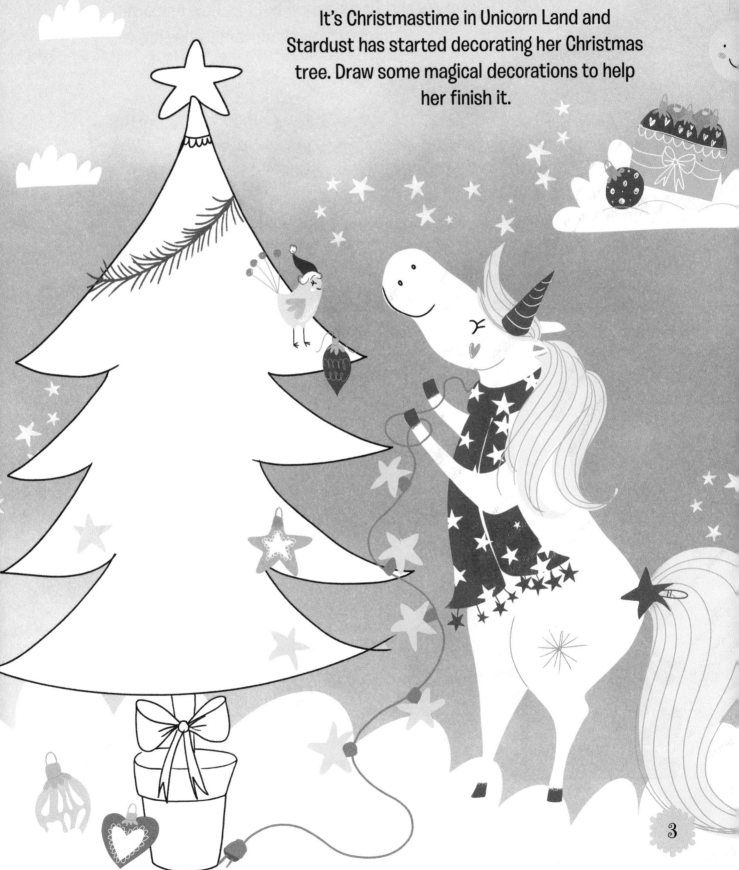

SNOW SHADOWS

Rainbow and Twinkle have built a snow unicorn!
Can you find and circle which shadow matches it exactly?

Friend Finder

Sparkle is writing her Christmas card list, and doesn't want to leave anyone out.
Can you help her find all her friends' names in the grid below?

STARDUST **SHIMMY** **RAINBOW** **CANDY** **TWINKLE**

SNOWY **GLITTER** **BEAUTY** **BELLE** **MISTY**

T	H	S	N	O	W	Y	E	N	L	Z	M
T	W	T	M	A	D	I	N	R	B	Q	G
W	P	A	I	Z	O	U	F	R	E	S	L
I	G	R	A	I	N	B	O	W	L	J	I
N	Z	D	H	C	U	S	V	O	L	B	T
K	H	U	L	K	D	H	C	Q	E	Z	T
L	B	S	Q	V	Y	I	N	B	P	S	E
E	I	T	G	D	P	M	W	M	Y	A	R
B	X	C	N	R	O	M	Q	I	E	Y	F
K	R	A	B	J	K	Y	T	S	V	P	W
I	C	U	E	K	G	F	X	T	M	J	O
L	S	P	B	E	A	U	T	Y	L	T	X

5

Creative Cards

Misty loves making her own Christmas cards to send to her family and friends. Draw your own Christmas card design below; then on the next page, write a nice message for the inside.

Dazzling Decorations

Rainbow wants to buy as many beautiful decorations as she can. She has 17 gold coins to spend. If she buys a star for her tree, how many ornaments can she afford?

_____ ornaments

stars:
5 gold coins

ornaments:
3 gold coins

Festive Lights!

Shimmy, Belle, and Twinkle have taken a trip into the Magic Village to look at the Christmas lights. They love how pretty it all is! Take a good look at the scene and then turn the page to answer some questions from memory.

Belle

Shimmy

Twinkle

Festive Lights! (continued)

See if you can answer these questions without peeking back.

1. Is Belle wearing a pink or purple scarf?

   ----

2. How many streetlights are in the picture?

   ----

3. Shimmy is looking in a store window. What does the store sell? --------------------------

4. True or false: There is a cat in the picture.

   ----

5. Twinkle is carrying a shopping bag. What has she bought?

   ----

6. Who or what is flying? --------------------------

Tinsel Tangle

The unicorns are decorating their Christmas trees, but their tinsel has become tangled! Can you figure out which unicorn is decorating which tree?

1. _____   2. _____   3. _____

Secret List

Merry loves making presents for her family and friends. Write a list of nice things you could make for all your loved ones at Christmas.

1 _____

2 _____

3 _____

4 _____

5 _____

ODD COOKIE

Candy has baked some Christmas gingerbread men, but one doesn't match! Can you find and circle which one it is?

Magic Market

The unicorns are having fun at the Cloudpark Christmas Market!
Add more colors to this magical scene.

14

Which Wands?

The unicorns' fairy friends cast lots of spells at Christmastime to make it as magical as possible. Can you find this exact sequence of wands in the grid below?

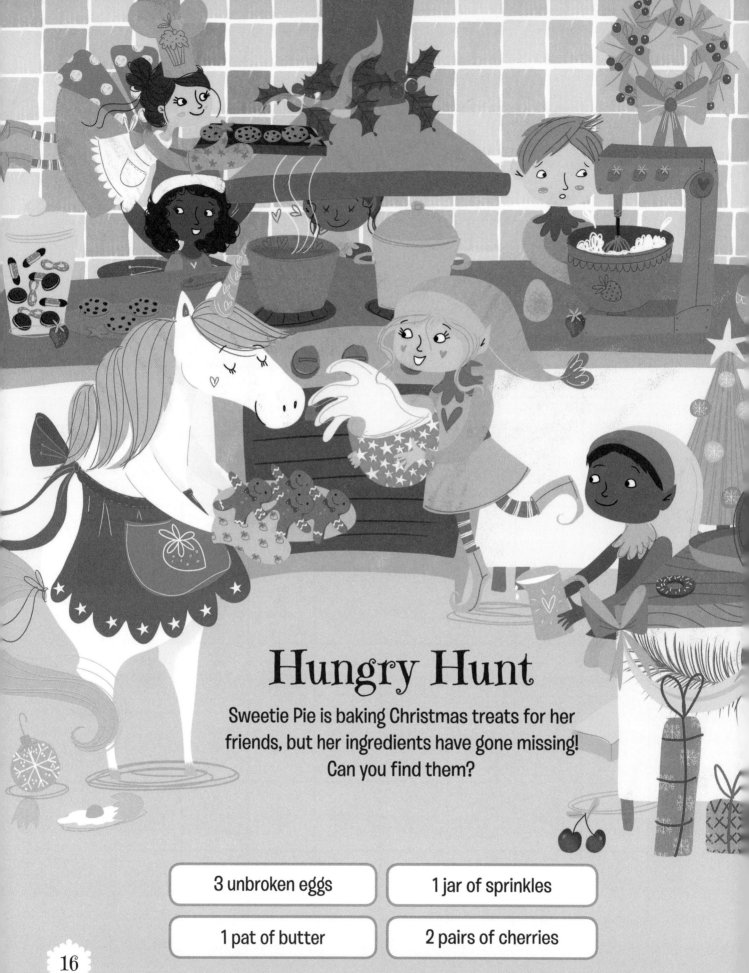

Hungry Hunt

Sweetie Pie is baking Christmas treats for her
friends, but her ingredients have gone missing!
Can you find them?

3 unbroken eggs

1 jar of sprinkles

1 pat of butter

2 pairs of cherries

16

YOU-NICORN!

What would your unicorn name be? Take the first letter of your name to find out!
You can see what your friends' names would be too.

A: Glitter
B: Twinkle
C: Merry
D: Snowy
E: Giggle
F: Icy
G: Dazzle
H: Sparkle
I: Happy
J: Pretty
K: Misty
L: Sweet
M: Beauty

N: Jolly
O: Moon
P: Charming
Q: Dainty
R: Shimmy
S: Glimmer
T: Flicker
U: Golden
V: Beauty
W: Holly
X: Starry
Y: Glow
Z: Sunny

MY NAME WOULD BE:

MY BEST FRIEND'S NAME WOULD BE:

Misty's Muddle!

Misty has wrapped presents for all of her friends, but she forgot to put labels on them! She's trying to find Stardust's gift. Can you solve the clues below to find out which one it is?

1. It isn't stripy.
2. It isn't the smallest one.
3. It has a bow.
4. The wrapping paper doesn't have a pattern.

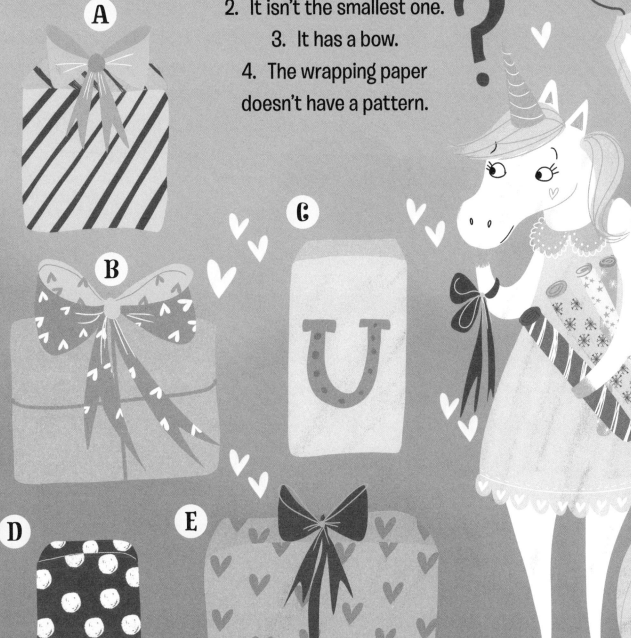

MOUNTAIN MAZE

Stardust wants to ski through the snow to her present in the middle.
Can you help her find the way?

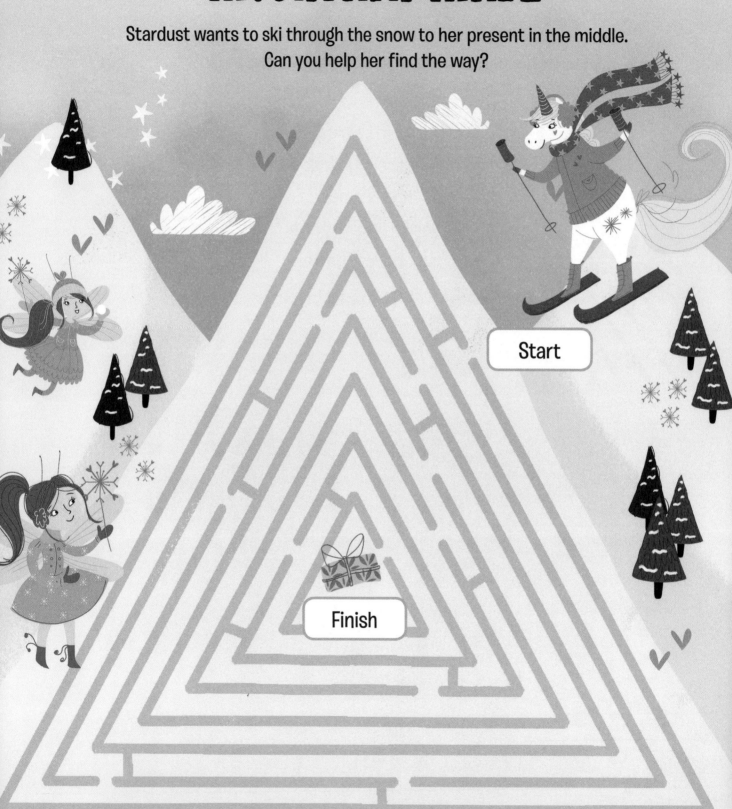

Start

Finish

Twinkle Toes

All the unicorns wear their best sparkly horseshoes at Christmas!
Beauty has lots, but they're in a muddle. Can you help match up all the pairs?

Work of Art

Twins Shimmy and Shiny love making snow unicorns at Christmastime. Can you spot eight differences between these two scenes? Circle the changes in the bottom picture.

Peeking In

Glitter has said nobody can come in while she wraps presents, but her curious little sisters are peeking! Can you find which jigsaw pieces complete the scene?

A

B

C

D

E

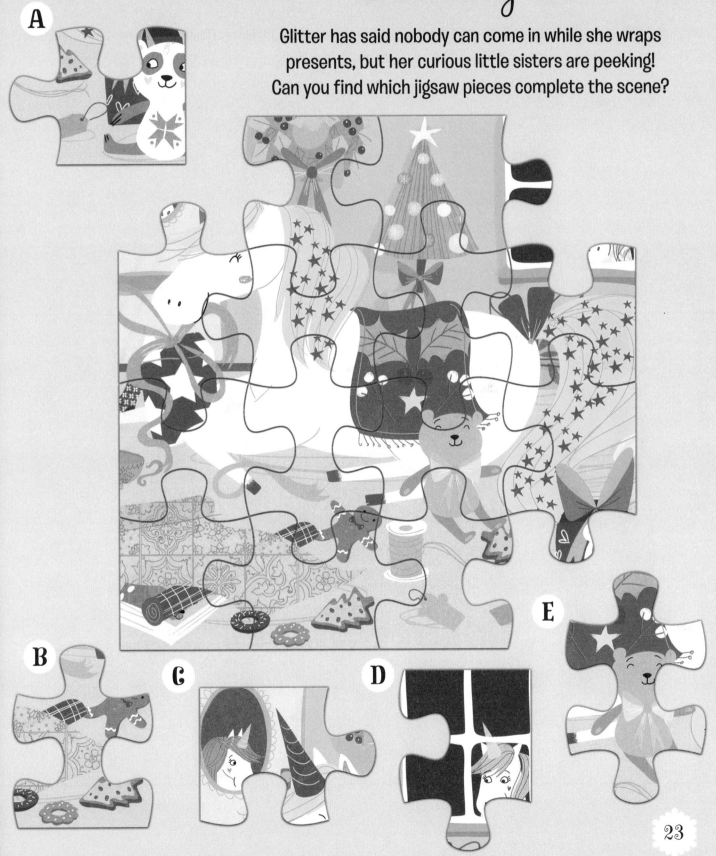

Sunny's Smoothies

It isn't winter everywhere: Sunny and her friends celebrate Christmas at the beach! Sunny has made fruity drinks to cool everyone down. Can you spot which one looks different?

Christmas Clues

Belle has made Dreamy a Christmas treasure hunt!
Help her follow the sprigs of holly to the special
Christmas present. She can move up, down, left, and
right, but not diagonally.

Start

Finish

Festive Fashion!

Everyone loves fun Christmas sweaters, especially the elves.
Decorate your own Christmas sweater, and be as creative as you like!

Toy Total

The Christmas fairies are packing up toys!
How many cute teddy bears can you count?

There are _____ teddy bears.

Game Time!

Oh no! Misty and Sparkle have spilled all the playing pieces
from their board game. The pieces come in pairs, except for one.
Find and circle the piece that doesn't have a match.

Singalong

At this time of year, the unicorns sing special Christmas songs together. Try making up one of your own. Here are some words to help you start:

Love

Candle

Presents

Snow

Hug

Holly

Tree

Glow

Drinks Order

Sparkle is the best at making delicious drinks in her coffee shop. Can you find these drinks in this exact order (from left to right) in the grid below?

Shining Bright!

Rainbow is very proud of her Christmas lights display.
Add more colors to make it look extra special.

Peaceful Dreams

Baby Gem is snuggling down in bed. Can you spot eight differences between these sleepy scenes? Circle the changes in the bottom picture.

Countdown!

Twinkle loves all of the yummy treats around at this time of year!
First, count the number of gingerbread men, and then the number of snowflake cookies.
Add them up to see how many days are left until Christmas!

	gingerbread men		snowflake cookies		days until Christmas
___		___		___	

Great Skates

The magic lake has completely frozen over, and everyone is out ice skating! Can you find these things hidden in the scene?

An owl

A snow mouse

3 lost mittens

An ice-skating fairy

2 pairs of green earmuffs

5 pine trees

Christmas Clothes

All the unicorns and their friends love getting dressed up in their special Christmas outfits. Draw an outfit you would love to wear on Christmas Day.

Pretty Mane

Candy loves to put sparkly hair clips in her mane when she goes to Christmas parties. Can you tell which type of hair clips she likes best? Hint: It's the one that appears the most in this picture.

Candy likes _____ hair clips best.

PERFECT PARTY!

It's Stardust's Christmas party! Ten baby fairies have sneaked out of bed to join in the fun. Can you circle them all?

Fir Forest

Misty and Belle are looking for the perfect Christmas tree. Solve the problems below, then add up the answers to find out which tree they should pick.

| 5 + 6 = | 17 - 15 = | 5 x 2 = | 11 - 4 = |

35

44

25

12

50

30

Special Stars

The unicorns love to go stargazing to spot all the shapes in the sky over Unicorn Land. Look carefully at this scene, then turn the page, and answer some questions from memory.

Special Stars (continued)

See if you can answer these questions without peeking back at the picture.

1. What shape is in the stars on the right of the picture? _____

2. How many shapes are in the stars altogether? _____

3. Which plant is in the stars? _____

4. How many unicorns are stargazing? _____

5. How many fairies are there? _____

Gorgeous Gifts

The best thing about Christmas is giving presents to family and friends. Can you find all the gifts the unicorns are giving this year?

SHOES   SCARF   TEDDY   NECKLACE

COMB   BOOK   BLANKET   PERFUME

I	C	W	N	S	V	R	K	N	N	D	A
G	B	J	Q	L	H	S	Y	B	E	G	R
T	S	Z	P	X	I	O	C	F	C	P	J
E	B	M	J	S	A	B	E	T	K	W	P
D	G	D	R	C	Q	S	E	S	L	S	K
D	Q	C	K	A	E	M	R	V	A	K	O
Y	N	X	F	R	U	J	C	D	C	H	O
T	K	F	T	F	Y	L	V	S	E	Z	B
X	W	P	R	W	E	C	O	M	B	E	U
M	H	E	Q	E	D	R	D	X	U	M	I
H	P	Z	L	O	B	L	A	N	K	E	T
L	H	Y	E	J	V	M	N	F	G	O	L

Christmas Creations

All of the Christmas unicorns have different types of magic. Look at the examples below, then draw and name your own Christmas unicorns!

1

Candy can make anything taste delicious! She loves making yummy treats for all her unicorn friends. Rainbow says that Candy even makes sprouts taste good!

2

Snowy can make snow fall and turn water into ice. She makes sure Unicorn Land is covered in pretty snow in time for Christmas!

44

This is ....

Her power is ....

This is ....

Her power is ....

Paper Patterns

Design your own Christmas wrapping paper. You can draw a repeating pattern, or simply doodle and let your imagination flow!

DAINTY DECORATIONS

Look at all these bright Christmas decorations.
Can you find the only matching pair?

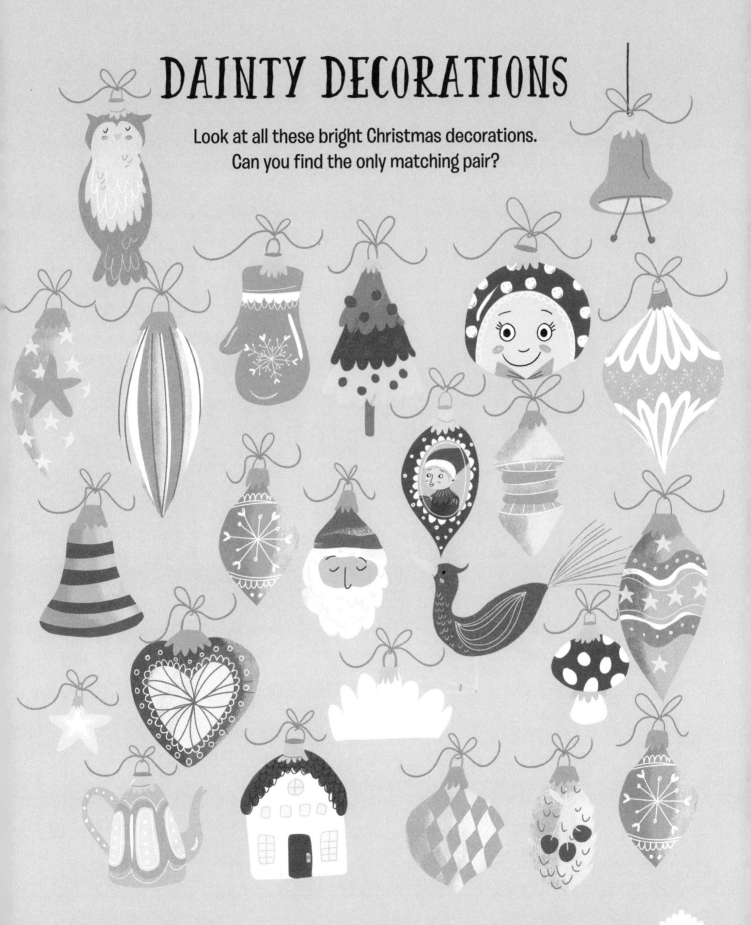

A Festive Fall

Snowy is using her magic to make fresh snowfall for Christmas!
Circle the jigsaw piece that completes the scene.

Frosty Snowflakes

Snow has now swept through Magic Land! Can you find a way back to the houses, following only the special snowflake? You can move up, down, left, and right, but not diagonally.

Start

Finish

All Bundled Up!

Candy and Shimmy are ready to go on a wintry walk.
Can you copy the picture of them onto the grid below?

Christmas Trinkets

Rainbow loves setting out her Christmas ornaments in a particular order. Can you find this exact sequence (from left to right) in the grid below?

Fairy Frolics

It's the fairy Christmas ballet!
Fill in this scene with more colors.

Cooking for Christmas

Glitter is getting ready to cook everybody a lovely Christmas Eve dinner. She has all the traditional unicorn treats—sparkle soup, candy crispies, rainbow puffs, and cloud cream! Write your own magical menu for a special Christmas Eve dinner with your friends.

STARTER

....

MAIN

....

DESSERT

....

DRINKS

....

Seasonal Songs

All the unicorns, elves, and fairies love singing Christmas
carols and playing their instruments together.
Can you find these instruments in the grid below?

FLUTE   CLARINET   PIANO   ORGAN   GUITAR
TRUMPET   DRUM   VIOLIN   TRIANGLE   OBOE

H	R	Y	W	M	J	R	I	O	B	O	E
P	P	C	H	N	P	D	F	R	T	G	C
G	U	I	T	A	R	Q	H	G	S	S	L
T	D	V	A	W	P	X	V	A	C	Y	A
R	H	G	Z	N	L	F	G	N	D	F	R
U	T	Y	X	P	O	D	S	J	R	V	I
M	T	R	I	A	N	G	L	E	M	I	N
P	S	T	Y	C	Z	E	Q	T	V	O	E
E	N	F	M	R	L	T	J	B	Z	L	T
T	W	U	J	S	X	U	K	Y	Q	I	K
O	R	E	L	C	Q	L	K	W	B	N	V
D	N	B	M	Z	N	F	D	G	L	M	L

Wrapping Tangle

These unicorns were all wrapping presents, but their pretty ribbons are now all tangled up!
Can you sort them out again to figure out who was wrapping each one?

1. _____   2. _____   3. _____

Festive Flowers

Stardust has made some beautiful Christmas wreaths!
Can you find the one that looks a little bit different?

Rainbow Rush

It's rainbow sledding time!
Can you untangle the twisted routes to
find out who won the race?

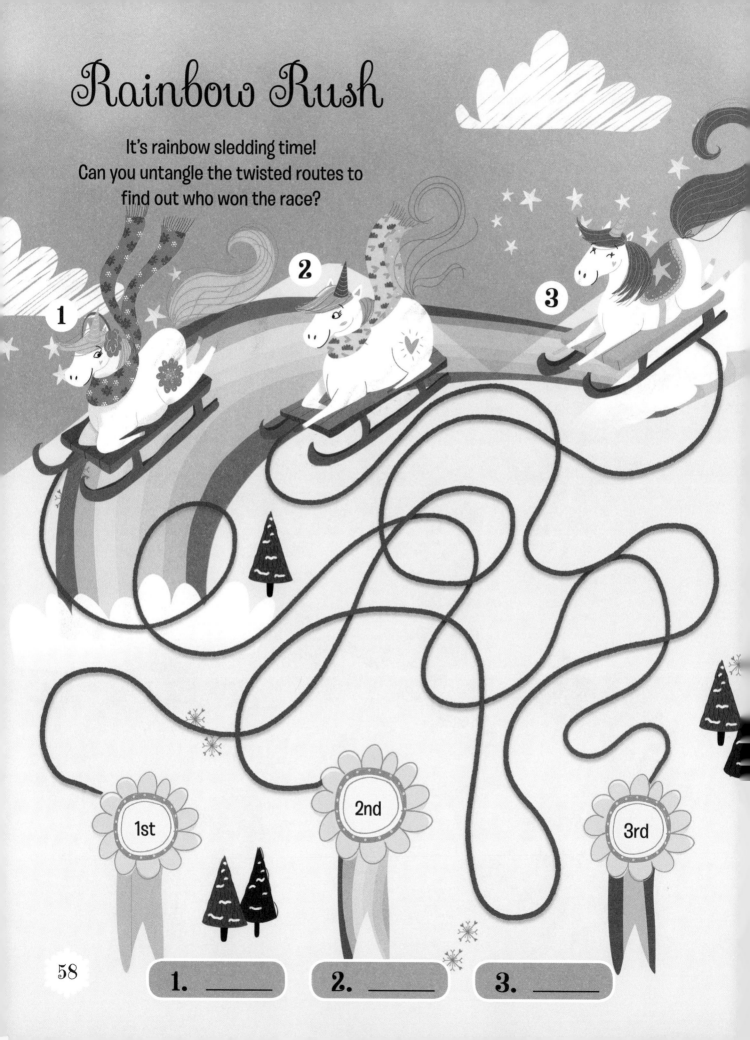

1. _____   2. _____   3. _____

Charade Shadow

Dreamy looks so funny playing charades at the Christmas Games night!
Can you find a shadow that matches her exactly?

Sock Swap

Cloudy knitted magical warming socks for her
elf friends, but now they're all jumbled up!
Can you match the finished ones back into pairs?

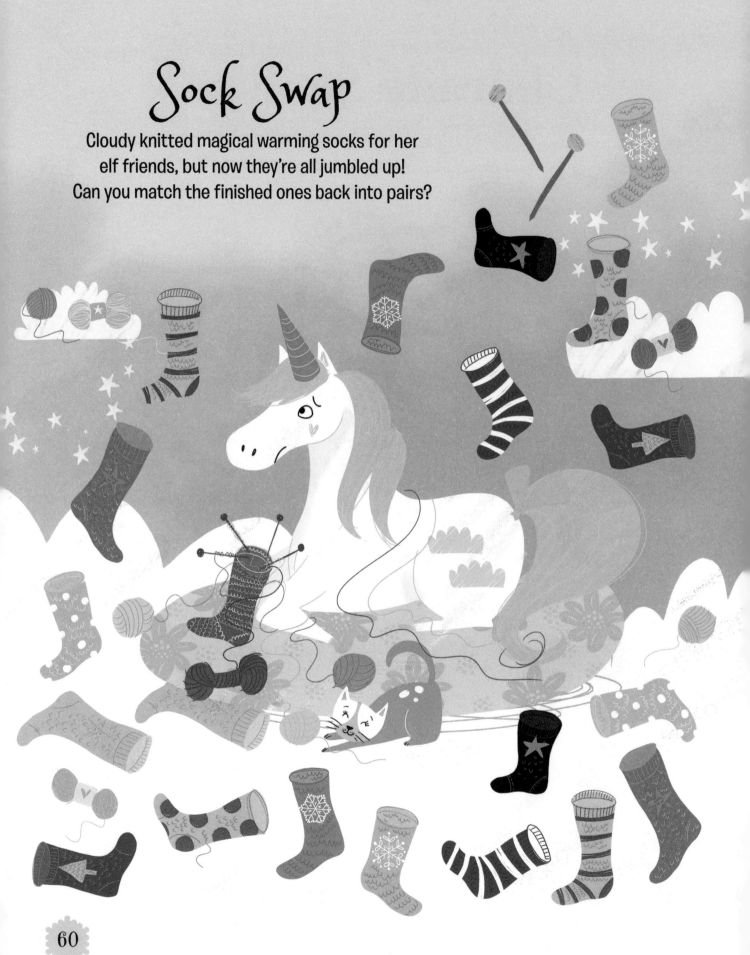

Magic Address Book

All the unicorns live in magical places.
Look at the cute unicorn addresses on this page, and then
try making up a magical address of your own!

Beauty
Perfect Cottage
Smiling Lane

Candy
Candlebright House
Star Street

Twinkle
Chocolate Cottage
Yummy Hill

Christmas Picnic!

It's pretty outside in the snow, so the unicorns are having a big Christmas feast! Finish coloring in this fun scene.

FLYING SNOWBALLS

The elves and fairies are having a big snowball fight!
Can you figure out where each jigsaw piece goes to complete the scene?

Special Delivery!

Glitter is helping Fern, the elf, deliver presents. Can you help Glitter follow Fern's footsteps through the grid? She can only move up, down, left, and right, not diagonally.

Finish

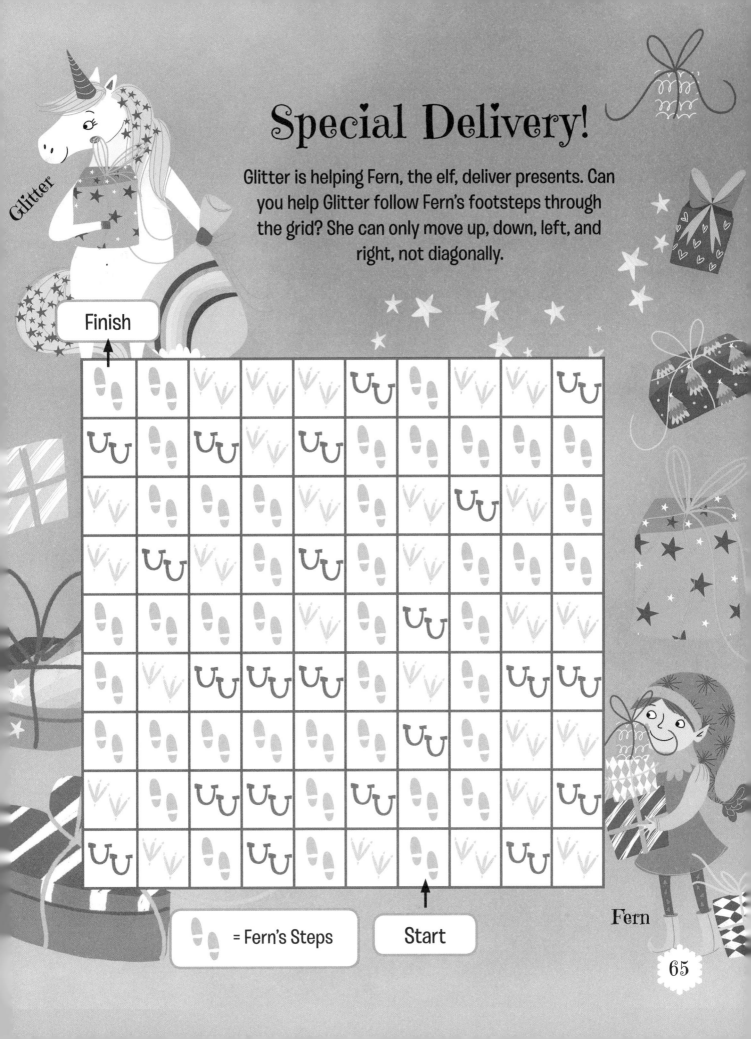

= Fern's Steps

Start

Fern

Party Time

Belle loves Christmas because there are so many fun parties!
This is the Christmas party look she likes best.
Can you re-create it in the grid?

Snowdrift Struggle

Stardust and Twinkle are on their way to a Christmas party. Can you help them find their way?

Start

Finish

GOT TO GIVE

What kind of Christmas gift giver are you?
Do the quiz below to find out.

1. If I had a big box of cookies to share with my friends, I would...

a. give them all away and not take any for myself.
b. put a nice little note with each one to make my friends smile.
c. send my friends on a fun treasure hunt to find the cookies!

2. When I go to a party, I...

a. always take a gift with me.
b. arrive early to help set up.
c. try to talk to everyone!

3. The best thing about Christmas is...

a. giving presents, of course!
b. spending time with my family and friends.
c. playing silly games together.

4. The best Christmas sweater is...

a. the one that matches with the one I got for my friend.
b. the one that was a special gift.
c. the one that lights up and plays tunes!

5. The best Christmas song is...

a. the one my family likes best.
b. the one that has the best lyrics.
c. the one that makes you want to dance.

6. The best Christmas outfit is...

a. one that someone has given you.
b. something interesting and unusual.
c. something bright and eye-catching.

MOSTLY As	MOSTLY Bs	MOSTLY Cs
GENEROUS	**THOUGHTFUL**	**EXCITING**
You like giving gifts to all of your family and friends, and you don't hold back at Christmas. You just like to spoil everyone!	You like to give presents that have a lot of meaning. Perhaps they are things you have made yourself or that you know mean a lot to the other person. They are always sweet and touch people's hearts!	You love to give weird and wonderful presents. The wackier the better! You like to surprise people, and Christmas Day with you is never dull!

Sunset Arrival

The unicorns' reindeer cousins have come to visit!
Finish coloring this magical sunset scene.

Flying Reindeer!

Here comes Jolly the reindeer!
Can you tell which picture of him is different?

Under the Sea

The Christmas mermaids are having a party.
Can you spot eight differences between these two scenes?
Circle the changes in the bottom picture.

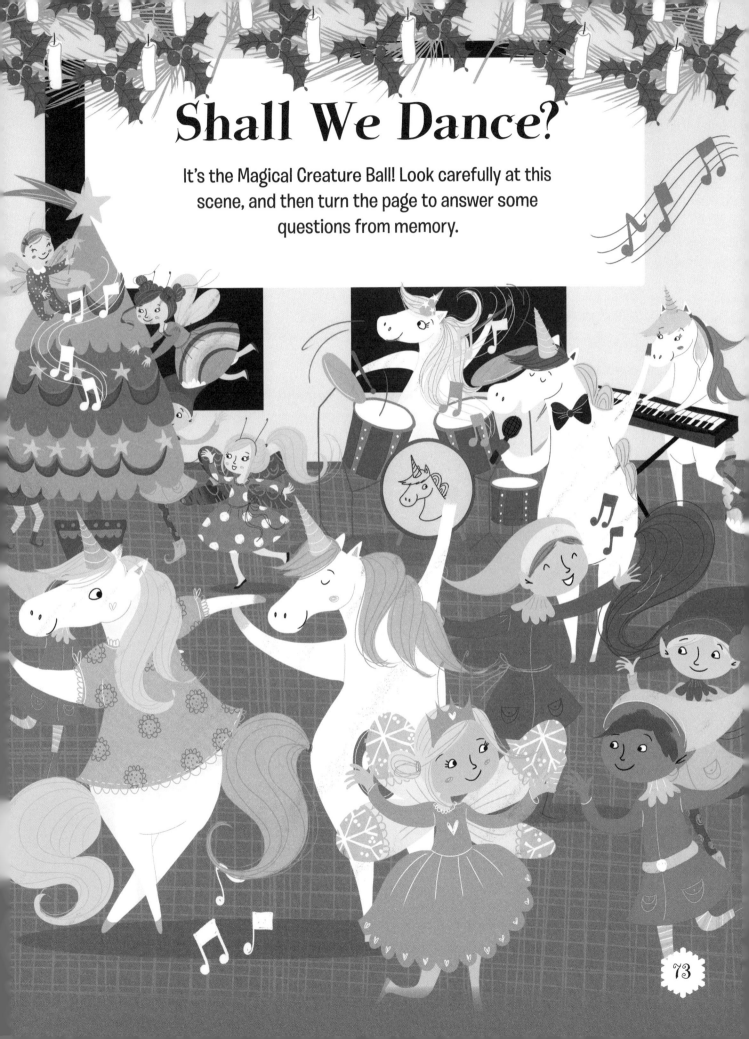

Shall We Dance?

It's the Magical Creature Ball! Look carefully at this scene, and then turn the page to answer some questions from memory.

Shall We Dance? (continued)

See if you can answer these questions!

1. How many creatures are wearing purple? ....

2. Are there drums in the picture? ....

3. What shape are the Christmas tree decorations? ....

4. Is anyone wearing a hat? ....

5. What is the baby fairy doing? ....

6. How many unicorns are singing? ....

Bird Buddies

Snowy likes to give Christmas presents to the birds!
Circle the little bird with a different number of tail feathers in this scene.

Workshop Whirl!

The Christmas elves are rushing to finish off all the presents in time!
Find and circle these three items in the main picture:

A doll with pigtails	A unicorn toy	A soft rabbit

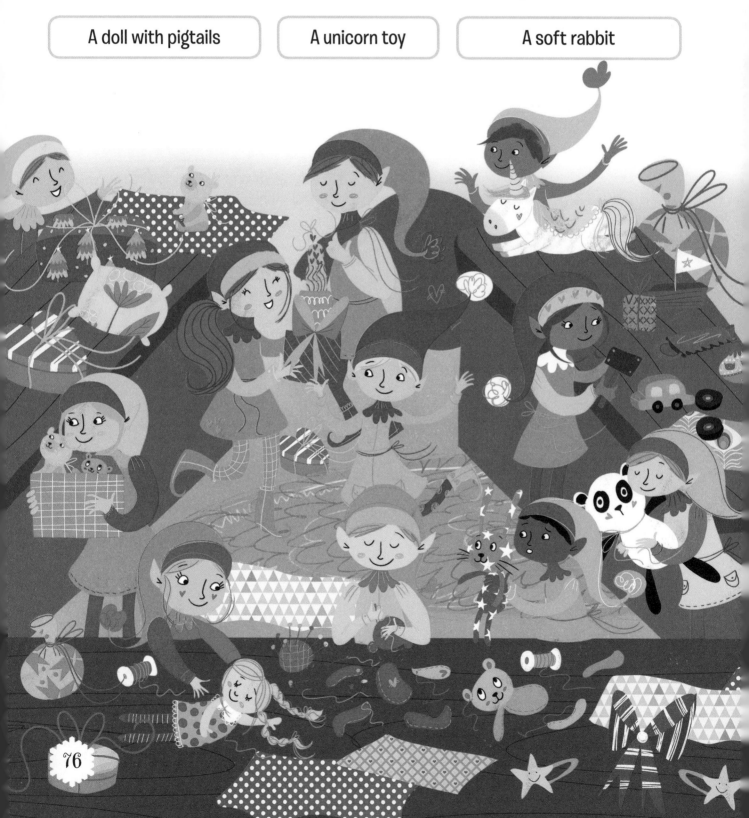

Bedtime Blues

Fairy Fiona has lost her teddy bear. She can't go to sleep on Christmas Eve without it. Which path will help her find it?

A

B

C

Doll

Teddy Bear

Train

FROZEN FLURRY!

All snowflakes are meant to be unique, but Glitter has found a matching pair!
Can you find and circle the two snowflakes that are the same?

Secret Santa

Dreamy has been given a beautiful ribbon in the Secret Santa exchange.
Can you figure out who her gift giver is?

1. There is no green on this unicorn.
2. She is not wearing a bow.
3. Her mane has a pattern.

A — Beauty

B — Sweetie Pie

C — Misty

D — Snowy

Dreamy

Winter Woods

Cloudy and Sweetie Pie have found a lost fairy in the wintry woods! Can you guide her home?

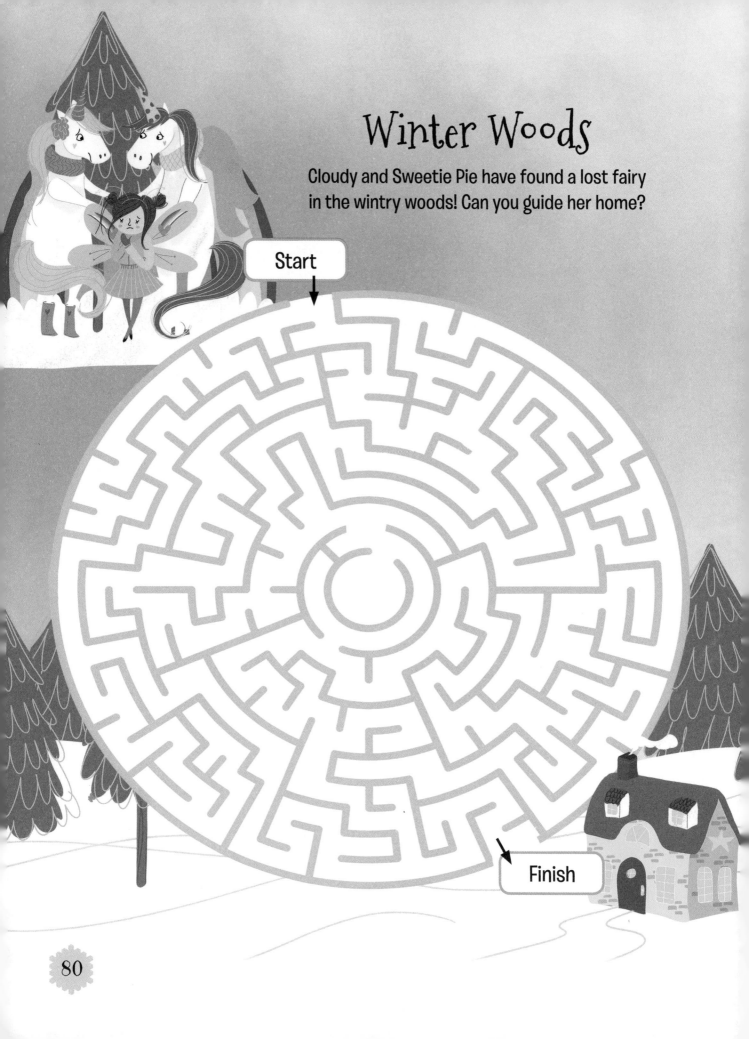

Start

Finish

Festive Breakfast

It's time for a Christmassy breakfast. Cute cupcakes all around! Decorate this plate with a Christmas pattern, then add some yummy food to eat.

Sleigh Ride

Santa Claus is letting the unicorns take a turn at pulling his sleigh.
Can you spot eight differences between the two pictures?
Circle the changes in the bottom scene.

FESTIVE FEAST

It's Christmas dinner time, and Candy has invited her friends over to eat.
Can you spot the plate that is missing something?

Jolly Jumble

Sparkle is choosing Christmas decorations for her home.
Find the four pieces that will complete the scene.

Present Time!

All the friends are opening their presents under the big Christmas tree!
Find and circle these things in the scene:

A little elf cuddling his new doll

A fairy helping tie a unicorn's tail bow

Two new horseshoes

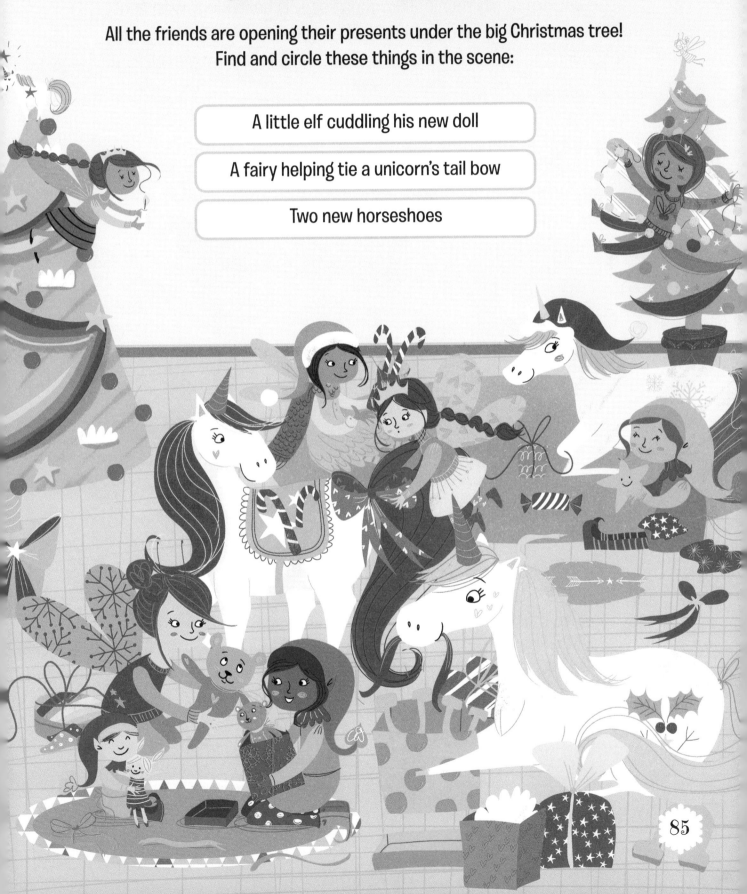

Reunicorn!

It's a unicorn family reunion! Grandpa Foggy is here, along with Aunty Moon, and all the unicorn cousins. Can you spot eight differences between the two scenes? Circle the changes in the bottom picture.

Magical Unicorn Christmas Activity Book

Answers

Answers

Page 4: Snow Shadows

Page 8: Dazzling Decorations

Rainbow can afford 4 ornaments.

Page 10: Festive Lights!

1. Purple
2. 5
3. Toys
4. True
5. Cupcakes
6. Fairies

Page 13: Odd Cookie

Page 5: Friend Finder

Page 11: Tinsel Tangle

1. B
2. C
3. A

Page 15: Which Wands?

Answers

Pages 16-17: Hungry Hunt

Page 22: Work of Art

Page 19: Misty's Muddle!

B

Page 21: Twinkle Toes

Page 23: Peeking In

Page 20: Mountain Maze

Answers

Page 24: Sunny's Smoothies

Page 27: Toy Total

There are 11 teddy bears.

Page 28: Game Time!

Page 25: Christmas Clues

Page 30: Drinks Order

Page 32: Peaceful Dreams

Page 33: Countdown!

3 gingerbread men
+ 4 snowflake cookies
= 7 days until Christmas

Answers

Pages 34-35: Great Skates

Page 37: Pretty Mane

Candy likes star hair clips best.

Pages 38-39: Perfect Party!

Page 40: Fir Forest

5 + 6 = 11

17 - 15 = 2

5 x 2 = 10

11 - 4 = 7

Final answer: 30

Page 42: Special Stars

1. A rainbow
2. 5
3. A Christmas tree/fir tree
4. 4
5. 3

Page 43: Gorgeous Gifts

I	C	W	N	S	V	R	K	N		N	D	A
G	B	J	Q	L	H	S	Y	B	E	E	G	R
T	S	Z	P	X	I	O	C	F	C	C	P	J
E	D	B	M	J	S	A	B	E	T	K	W	P
D	G	D	R	C	Q	S	E	S	L	L	E	A
D	Q	C	K	A	E	M	R	V	A	A	E	K
V	N	X	F	R	U	J	C	D	C	C	Z	O
T	K	F	T	F	Y	L	V	S	E	E	O	O
X	W	P	R	W	E	C	O	M	B	E	U	B
M	H	E	Q	E	D	R	D	X	U	M	I	
H	P	Z	L	O	B	L	A	N	K	E	T	
L	H	V	E	J	V	M	N	F	G	O	L	

Answers

Page 47: Dainty Decorations

Page 49: Frosty Snowflakes

Page 55: Seasonal Songs

Page 48: A Festive Fall

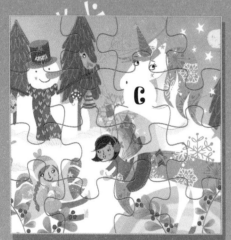

Page 51: Christmas Trinkets

Page 56: Wrapping Tangle

1. C
2. B
3. A

Page 57: Festive Flowers

Answers

Page 58: Rainbow Rush

1. 3rd
2. 2nd
3. 1st

Unicorn 3 won the race.

Page 59: Charade Shadow

Page 60: Sock Swap

Page 64: Flying Snowballs

Page 65: Special Delivery

Page 67: Snowdrift Struggle

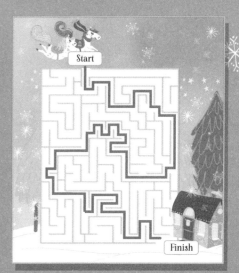

Page 71: Flying Reindeer!

Answers

Page 72: Under the Sea

Page 75: Bird Buddies

Page 77: Bedtime Blues

A. Train
B. Teddy Bear
C. Doll
Path B leads to the Teddy Bear.

Page 78: Frozen Flurry!

Page 74: Shall We Dance?

1. 4
2. Yes
3. Stars
4. Yes
5. Decorating the tree
6. 1

Page 76: Workshop Whirl!

Page 79: Secret Santa

D. Snowy

Answers

Page 80: Winter Woods

Page 83: Festive Feast

Page 85: Present Time!

Page 82: Sleigh Ride

Page 84: Jolly Jumble

Page 86: Reunicorn!

Have a magical
Christmas!